G. H. Walker

Home and Country

G. H. Walker

Home and Country

ISBN/EAN: 9783337428129

Printed in Europe, USA, Canada, Australia, Japan

Cover: Foto ©Andreas Hilbeck / pixelio.de

More available books at **www.hansebooks.com**

HOME AND COUNTRY,

A MILITARY DRAMA,

IN FIVE ACTS.

BY G. H. WALKER.

Author of "THE OLD FLAG; OR, THE SPY OF NEWBERN."

HARTFORD, CONN.
SOLDIERS' RECORD STEAM PRINT.
1871.

DRAMATIS PERSONÆ.

FEDERALS.

JOHN MARSHALL.
JERRY JOWLER.
MIKE DONOVAN.
WILLIE DONOVAN.
GENERAL, COMMANDING.
SURGEON OF THE ARMY.
CAPT. WINSLOW.
SERGT. BATES.
COMPANY K.
HOSPITAL CORPS.

CONFEDERATES.

EDWARD MARTIN.
JAMES McDONALD.
LIEUT. WHITE.
SERGT. JACKSON.
THE RAVEN WINGS.

LADIES.

MRS. MARSHALL.
KATE DONOVAN.
MINNIE MARSHALL.

HOME AND COUNTRY.

ACT I.

Scene 1.—*A scantily furnished room.*—Minnie *discovered on a lounge* c, *with her mother tending her.*—*Curtain rises slowly to music.*

Mrs. M. Don't you feel better now, darling ?

Minnie. No, Mother, I believe I am growing worse. Oh ! Oh ! (*Hands on her side.*) Isn't there anything you can give me, Mother ? Something warm to drink I think would relieve me.

Mrs. M. There is nothing in the house, Minnie, to make hot drinks. No fire to warm anything for you. I expect Willie home soon, and if Mr. Howard lets him have the money he wants, he will go and get something that will help you.

Minnie. Mother, do you suppose that Father takes Willie's money away from him to buy liquor with ? Maggie Burns told me so the other day. But I don't believe it, do you ?

Mrs. M. I don't know. I am afraid that he does. Your father is not the man that he used to be.

Minnie. He was real kind to us once, wasn't he ? And if it wasn't for drink he would be just as good now.

1*

(*Enter* KATE DONOVAN, R *with small basket.*)

Mrs. M. Oh, Mrs. Donovan, I am glad you have called.

Kate. (*Going up to Minnie*) How is the little darling to-night?

Mrs. M. She don't seem to be any better, nor I haven't any thing in the world to give her.

Kate. Its meself, Mrs. Marshall, that can truly sympathize with you, for I have been through it all. I expected how it was. So I brought some cordial, and it is just what-she needs. It will make her sleep.

Mrs. M. I know that is what she wants. She hasn't closed her eyes for three days. It isn't anything that will hurt her, is it?

Kate. No, it has been used in the family for years. The doctors never object to it. I don't know that it cures, but it quiets the nerves and gives sleep when one has been long without it.

Mrs. M. Do you want to take some of it, Minnie?

Minnie. Oh yes, for I know it is just what I want. Mrs. Donovan, you are very kind.

(*Music.. They give her the cordial, her mother fans her till she sleeps.*)

Mrs. M. I never saw anything like that before.

Kate. You must have some rest yourself, Mrs. Marshall, or you will be down sick. Here is something for you to eat. (*Goes to the Basket.*)

Mrs. M. Mrs. Donovan, I am afraid you are robbing yourself.

Kate. No, no, not a bit. I know it is not much of this world's goods that I have, and it's a hard time that I have to get along, for Mike is still idling away his time, and drinking worse than ever.

But I manage better since little Maggie died, for now I have both hands free to work, and leave Mike to shift for himself. Not a taste of food that I earn does he get. The only way I can get work out of him is to starve him to it. Its hard sometime to hear him beg for food when I know he is almost dying for it, but I always hold out for I know it would be best for him. I have tried to persuade him to go to the war; but he says he'll have nothing to do with the blasted "nager war" as he calls it. I sometimes think that if he *would* go it would make a man of him.

Mrs. M. Oh it seems dreadful to me to go there. And I am so fearful lest Willie may take it into his head to go. He says nothing about it, but he talks a great deal about the war, and if there ever was a little patriot Willie Marshall is one. And little Minnie there is just as patriotic as he, and her expressions of love for our country come from her heart with such fervency. She often asks her father why he does not go and fight for his country. He takes little notice of it, and there is not much danger of his going. It might do him good. But bad as he is, I would hate to have him go. Ah, what a change there has been in that man! It was just eighteen years ago this very month that he delivered his valedictory at Harvard College. With what pride I listened to his eloquent words. Oh, how he has changed! how he has fallen!

Kate. There, Mrs. Marshall, you should not let your mind run that way, it will make you sick entirely. Why don't you eat some of this?

Mrs. M. I don't want it now, I rather leave it till Willie comes. He will need it more than I.

(*Enter* MIKE DONOVAN, R. *His appearance in-
dicates that he has just come from a bloody fight in
the street.*)

Mike. Arrah, Katie, me darling, so I've found
ye at last. Sure its all over the neighborhood that
I've been hunting for ye. Its a little bit of a
scrimmage that I've been having in the strate. It
would have made yer heart lape with pride Katie
to see the way I walked into the fight. And it
was the most elegent victory ye ever seen.
Whoop! but isn't Mike Donovan the boy for givin
them a left handed cut under the right ear. But
sure the exercise has given me such an appetite as
was niver given to Alexander for bating the whole
world. But divil a bit could I find to eat in the
house. So come home now, me darling; you wont
refuse yer darling Mike a crust of bread, after the
glorious achavement he has won.

Kate. Mike Donovan, its ashamed of yerself
that ye ought to be, to be begging food of me and
able to lick a whole crowd in the strate. Go earn
the money and buy the food and I'll cook it for ye.

Mike. Sure Kate, its yerself as well as me that
knows that there is no work at all at all that I can
get to do None but a crazy man would think of
giving Mike Donovan a job now.

Kate. I know where ye can get a job, Mike,
and noble work it is too. Its only a little fighting
that ye'll have to do, and you like that, you know,
better than eating.

Mike. So its into that blasted nager war ye
would have me go. Faith I'll go and enlist this
minute.

Kate. (*detaining him*) No, no, Mike, dont go, I
was only fooling with ye. Would ye go way off

there and get killed, and leave yer poor Kate a widow.

Mike. Thin will ye give me something to ate?

Kate. Now Mike ye shouldn't take advantage of me so.

Mike. Then ye'll not give me anything to ate. Sure I must enlist then, or I'll starve.

Kate. No, no you mus'nt. Only don't leave me alone, Mike, and bad as ye are I'll work with me own hands to keep ye. I'd go home and get ye something to eat now, but there isn't a bit in the house. I brought the last morsel here in that basket.

Mike. (*looking into the basket*) Faith here is jist a nice lunch for me. (*Is going to take some food.*)

Kate. Mike Donovan, don't you dare to touch that. Would ye rob these poor starving cratures?

Mike. How the divil was I to know they're starving. Faith I'll enlist now.

Kate. Mike ye act like a brute, and its ashamed of ye that I am. Isn't there a spark of the man left in ye? Have ye forgotten the time that little Maggie was sick? How a kind woman came to us with food, and stayed with us all through the long dark night, until the angels took our little darling home? Do you remember how we thanked her with tears in our eyes? What that lady did for us, I have been doing for the family of John Marshall to-night.

Mike. John Marshall! did ye say John Marshall? And is this the wife and child of John Marshall? Oh, Mike Donovan, what if ye had done the mane trick ye were about to do? Faith I wish I was starving ten times worse than I am now, that I might kape this food from my own lips famishing

for its nade and give it for the relief of the family
of John Marshall. Ah, Kate, ye have done a noble
dade of charity, and I feel as if I had a hand in it
meself. It makes me heart beat once more like
the heart of a man. Come, Kate, let us go home
now; I can't bear to look at the sick child yonder.
It makes me think of little Maggie.

Kate. Good night, Mrs. Marshall, I suppose
Willie will be home soon, and if I am wanted, be
sure and send for me.

(*Music. Exit* KATE *and* MIKE.)

Mrs. M. Poor Minnie! How quick she breathes;
and she sleeps so soundly. I dont like to see her
that way.

(*A knock at the door,* R. *Mrs. Marshall rises
and opens it.*

Jerry. (*Outside.*) Does Mrs. Marshall live here,
she that was Mary Longley?

Mrs. M. Yes, Sir.

Jerry. (*Entering.*) Be you Mary?

Mrs. M. I suppose I am, sir.

Jerry. Ye don't say so. (*Shakes her hand vio-
lently.*) Why, Mary, ye don't know how glad I am
to see ye Don't ye know who I be?

Mrs. M. No, I don't seem to remember you.

Jerry. Wall, I swan, if that don't beat all
natur. Why, I knew you the minit I sot eyes on
ye. Look right straight at me, now. Can't ye remember?

Mrs. M. No, Sir.

Jerry Why, I'm yer cousin, Jerry Jowler.
(*Shakes her hand again*) Now, I guess ye know
who I be, don't ye? Ain't quite forgot Jerry,
have ye?

Mary. Can it be possible? Oh! Jerry, you don't know how glad I am to see you.

Jerry. Wall, you better believe that I'm some glad to see you. Is that your child?

Mrs. M. Yes, and she is very sick.

Jerry. Seems to me she's sleeping amazing sound for a sick gal. I shouldn't like to have her that way, no how, if she's mine.

Mrs. M. She has not slept for a long time, and I think that she will be better for it when she awakes. But take a chair, Jerry, I want to hear something about the old place. I haven't heard a single word from there since I left. I never expected to see you down here.

Jerry. Wall, it is somewhat remarkable that I should get so far from hum. But the pesky doin's of them ere tarnal rebs has jest set my blood to bilin like all possessed; so ye see I come down here to the city to see if I can't get a chance to go.

Mrs. M. You will find opportunities enough here, for men are being enlisted by the hundreds every day. But is there no chance for enlisting in the country?

Jerry. Wall, yes; but ye see I didn't find a chance that jest suited me. They raised a company up there to hum, and I jined, and they promised to make me leftenant. But when election come, I'll be blamed if I got a single vote. And then to smooth it all over, what does the captin do but come and offer me the position of first corporal. You better believe my dander riz higher nor a kite. They couldn't smooth things over with no such soft sodder as that. So ye see I jest *on*-listed, to let the darned fools have things all their own way. I was bound to go somewhere and see if I couldn't be appreciated. But I tell ye what, I'm patriotic as thunder, and getting to be more and more so every day, and I shouldn't wonder a darn bit but what I got so excited yet that I'd jest up and enlist, if I didn't get nothing higher nor an orderly sergeant. That's so, by lightning.

Mrs. M. Well, Jerry, I am glad to see you so patriotic, and hope you will win lots of glory. But there is one thing that I wish to speak to you about. It is in regard to Willie, my oldest child. He is nothing but a mere boy, but I am afraid he has some thoughts of going to the war, and I don't want you to give him the least encouragement. He is all I have to lean upon now, and I believe it would kill me were he to go. Oh, Jerry! you don't know what I have suffered since I saw you last. I must tell you all about it. It isn't much to tell, though—the same old story of stimulants, intoxication, debauchery and ruin. John Marshall, once so proud and noble, is only a miserable wreck.

Jerry. Wall, I swan, if this doesn't beat all natur, and he had sich all-fired nice larnin, and could make sich all killing big speeches.

Mrs. M. There never was a young man who entered upon his profession with brighter prospects than he. When I think of it, it does not seem possible. Here I am, Jerry, upon the very verge of starvation, and little Minnie sick, so terrible sick, with nothing in the world to relieve her. In this basket is the only food that has been in the house for three days, and a kind Irish lady, almost as poorly off as I, just brought it here. I am keeping it for Willie. He will be home from the store soon. He said he should try and get some money from his employer, but I am afraid he will not, for he has already taken up more than he has earned. They say that John takes the money away from him to spend for liquor. And what is more terrible than all, he has lately come home in a dreadful passion, and had it not been for the restraining influence of little Minnie, he would have beaten me, perhaps killed me. It is strange, the power that Minnie has over him.

Jerry. (*Rising Excitedly*) The blasted mean contemptible skunk, I'd jest like to catch him raising a hand agin you. It's a darned shame anyhow and ye hadn't orter live with him another day under no sarcumstances whatsumever. If I'd only a known jest how things was, I could a helped ye jest as well as not, and been mighty glad to done it. You don't know how much I used to think of ye, Mary. Mebby ye wouldn't believe it, but jest as true as I stand here, I cried like a baby when I hearn ye was married. I'd a given the last cent I had in the world rather than to see ye suffer like this. But it isn't too late to help ye now. It'll be easy enough to get rid of yer husband after what he has done, and then I'll see that ye don't want for nothin' no more. It wouldn't do much good to try to do anything for ye with him hanging around beatin' on ye, and stealing all that was gin ye, to buy liquor with. So the first thing you do is to apply for a divorce, and get rid of the critter right off. I'll stand the expense, by thunder.

Mrs. M. I thank you very much, Jerry, for your kind intentions, but you have advised me to do that which Mary Marshall scorns to give one moment's thought. I know that John is very low, that he treats me very cruelly. But he is the same John Marshall to whom I vowed at the marriage

2

altar to be faithful unto death. And though he be
ten times more degraded, ten times more brutal, I
shall hold the marriage compact as an ordinance of
God and keep it sacred to the end. While he lives
—and I fear it may not be long—I am his wife,
and for the sake of what he has been, if no more, I
shall deem it my duty, aye, a pleasure, to share
with him all dishonor and degradation.

Jerry. (*Aside.*) I've read about jes sich wimmin as her in story books, but darn me if I ever
seen one afore. Taint no sorter wonder that I
used to love that ar gal almost to-death. It came
deuced near spiling me.—I'm afraid I shall have
another spell on it now.

(*Enter Willie.*)

Mrs. M. Willie this is our cousin, Jerry Jowler.

Jerry. How do you do, William? I'm proper
glad to see ye.

Willie. How is Minnie? She has gone to sleep
hasn't she?

Mrs. M. Yes, Mrs. Donovan has been here and
given her some cordial that made her sleep. Did
you get any money from Mr. Howard?

Willie. No, mother. He said he could not let
me have any more money until I had earned it.
Mother, there is something that I have thought a
great deal of doing, but I have never spoken to you
about it. I want to be a soldier, and do what little
I can to help save the Union, that is now threaten-
ed with so much danger. If things had been different with us, I should have gone before this.

Mrs. M. Oh Willie, you must not go; it will
break my heart if you do.

Willie. I do hate to leave you, mother, but others
have given up their sons. By going I can help

you more than I do now. My pay will be greater
and it can be arranged so that you can get state aid.
You will let me go, wont you, mother? I must
have some share in this noble work.

Mrs. M. It makes my heart beat with pride to
hear you talk thus. But you know, darling, that
misfortune has made you doubly dear to me. After
all I have suffered it don't seem as if it could be my
duty to make this sacrifice.

Willie. Mother, there is no sacrifice too great
for our country. I know the parting will be hard
mother, but I believe it will be for the best.

Mrs. M. (*In her chair sobbing*) Oh! don't talk
about it any more, I can't endure the thought. Oh
merciful God, why am I thus afflicted.

Jerry. Mebby as how I aint no sorter buisness
to put my yap in here, but then on the other hand
it may be doin my country a sarvice to spit out jes
what I've made up my mind to. Now its jest as
plain as a nose on a man's face, that that are boy
has got patriotism bilin into every part of him.
We read a good deal about sich things in the news-
papers, but its plaguey seldom that ye see love for
Uncle Sam shown up life size as it is there. Now
folks may talk about the curse of slavery and the
galling chains that are hitched onto the groaning
nigger. I know its allfired sickening, and makes a
fellow's blood bile to think on, but I believe its
slavery ten hundred thousand million times worse
and more, to take the slimsiest string, it dont make
no darned odds if its what they call the silken cord
of love, and fetter the arm that is fired with patriotism and raised to strike in defense of liberty.
Ye may love that are boy, Mary, but his country
has got the first claim on him, and I believe if ye

let him be guided by the noble spirit that freedom has planted into his breast, somehow in the ways of Providence, a blessing will come to ye. Now ye see I've got some dosh in this old wallet and I put it there to spend for the good of my country. I made up my mind to do it, and no human critter can't stop me. I thought as mebby I'd have to hunt some time before I could find a good chance, but it come a darn sight quicker than I expected. Ye can't make no excuse now, Mary, I'll enlist and go right along with him, and ye shall have every thing to hum that ye want.

Willie. Oh, Cousin Jerry, you don't know how much I thank you. Now mother, you will let me go, wont you?

Mrs. M. (*deeply moved.*) Yes, Willie, if you will promise me one thing. You know what has ruined your father. I see more danger for you in this than in the deadly bullet. Now for your life, Willie, don't ever touch a drop of liquor.

Willie. Mother, I promise you this, and God knows that my mind is already firmly fixed. Come mother, don't weep. You should rejoice that you have a son to give in this glorious cause

Jerry. Wall Willie, its my opinion that ye better go right out and get something for the comfort of the house. Here's some money. But the first thing ye do, get a doctor. I don't like the looks of that little gal, no how.

Willie. Poor Minnie, I'll be back soon, (*Exit* R.)

Jerry (*Hesitatingly*) I hope Mary ye wont feel delicate nor nothing about taking the money I'm going to give ye as a sort of a bounty for Willie. I know that wimmin are some times gol darned particular about sich things. 'Twas meaner than soap-grease for me to say what I did to ye about leaving yer husband. But darn it all, you know jest how that is without me tellin on yer. Now ye wont refuse it, will ye?

Mrs. M. (*Rising.*) No, Jerry, for I believe you give it with the best of motives. Ah! Jerry, old friends, the friends of youth, the friends that have shared our childish joys and sorrows, are the true friends, after all!

(*Enter* JOHN MARSHALL.)

John. Got anything to eat here? If you haven't, there'll be a devil of a row.

· *Mrs. M.* Hush, John, Minnie is sleeping.

John. It's all your own fault, having her sick that way. If you had half taken care of her, she'd have been well before this. What ye standing there for? why the devil don't you fly round and get me something to eat? (*Sees* JERRY.) Hullo! who the devil is this? Here's a go, the old woman's got a feller. I say, Mary, can't ye give a feller an introduction?

Mary. It is my cousin, Jerry Jowler.

John. How do you do, Mr. Growler? I'm delighted to see you, Mr. Chousler, I mean *Cousin* Frowsler. I am exceedingly honored with your visit. Hope I ain't kept you waiting long.

Jerry. John Marshall, if you've got the remotest idee into your head that I come here to see you, all I've got to say is that you are teetotally and everlastingly mistaken.

John. If ye didn't come to see me, who the devil did ye come to see?

Jerry. Your wife.

John. Oh, ye did, did ye? Well then, Mr.

2*

Grizzly, all I've got to say is, that the sooner you get out of this the better.

Jerry. I don't think I shall leave for you, you dirty, miserable, drunken critter. You conglomerated diabolical compound double extract of the essence of meanness.

John. You won't leave, hey? Then all I've got to do is to put ye out myself.

Jerry. There never wa'n't no John Marshall made nor never will be through all coming eternity, that's got the muscle onto him that's capable of putting one side of me through a forty foot door.

Music. JOHN *grapples* JERRY. *They struggle, and* JERRY *is forced out* R. *Mary kneels beside Minnie.*

John. Now, Mary, we'll see about this. (*Is going to strike* MARY, *when Minnie suddenly starts up and arrests the blow. Music chords.* TABLEAU.

Enter WILLIE, R., *with bundles, &c.* MINNIE *sinks back.* JOHN *and* MARY *turn to* WILLIE, *who lays things on the table, and hesitatingly approaches his father.*

Willie. Father, did you know that I was going to the war?

John. What ye talking about, ye little fool. You ain't old enough nor big enough.

Willie. There are a great many as small as I that are going. Capt. Winslow has agreed to take me.

John. It don't make any difference, you can't go without my consent. I don't believe there's any justice in carrying on this war, and I am not going to help sustain it. So that's the long and short of that matter.

Minnie. (*Awaking.* Did you say that you were going to the war, Willie? It is a noble resolution, and makes me so proud of you. It is such a privilege to be able to serve our country, when it is in danger. I wouldn't have mother suffer by your going, but I know that God will provide for her. Father, I wish you were going with him. What is the reason, father, that you care so little about your country? I have something here that I am going to give you, father. It is some manuscript that I found in the old trunk up stairs. It is about love of home and country, and has such beautiful thoughts, I have read it over and over again. Father, I am not going to be with you much longer, for death is very near to me, and I thought you might read this if I gave it as a dying gift. (*Gives the manuscript, and sinks back.*)

John. It is my writing! The Oration delivered with my Valedictory! Oh! that wasn't this John Marshall, this miserable, degraded sot, with no more feeling than a brute. (*Sinks into a chair, l. WILLIE stands by* MINNIE.)

Mrs. M. What is it, John? (*Takes the manuscript.*) "Home and Country." I do not wonder, John, that the memory of this overpowers you. It was not the practical application of these thoughts that has darkened our home and destroyed our country's peace.

John. Oh! those words come back to me like a flame of fire, kindling into life those emotions that have so long slumbered. Oh! what have I been! What have I done! It wasn't I that did it. It wasn't I that brought misery and starvation to this once happy home. It was that cursed drink. That monster that robs men of their senses, and makes them worse than brutes. But then it is my fault. Didn't I yield myself a willing tool to do its hellish work. (*Rises.*) But I will be its slave no more, so help me God!

Music. MRS. M. *sinks into a chair*, R. WILLIE *goes up to her, and receives her embrace.* JOHN *looks at them and then kneels by* MINNIE.

John. Oh, if Minnie would only live now, all might be redeemed. How still and deathlike. Cold drops on her forehead, and her hands are like ice. It is too late, the touch of death is on her. Oh, if she could only speak to me once more!

Minnie. Oh, it was so beautiful! I saw it only a moment, but long enough to see that our cause was upheld in Heaven.—You will read that, won't you, Father, and follow its teachings?

John. Oh, Minnie! every one of those words were written by my hand, and came from the very depth of my soul. All this wonderful love that you have for your country, was inherited from me. And now, Minnie, if what you just saw be the bright realms of Heaven where you are going, bear with you the message that John Marshall is consecrated forever to his country's cause.

Minnie. Oh, Father, you have made me so happy. Come, mother, kiss me, I'm going. (*Music.*) Willie—father—I have done something for freedom, haven't I, father, for I have led you back to its altar, and I shall soon see the bright angels there rejoice.

Points up. Music. Other characters kneel by MINNIE. *Allegory discovered—"The Altar of Freedom."* TABLEAU.

END OF ACT I.

ACT II.

SCENE.—*Landscape.—Two small tents at back.—
Arms stacked in front.*

Fife and drum sound the reveille.—Enter ORDERLY
SERGEANT, R.

Ord. (*Putting his head in the first tent.*) Turn
out to roll call. (*Repeats at next tent and three
times off,* L.

JERRY JOWLER, MIKE DONOVAN, *and soldiers
turn out of tents, and others enter* R. *and* L., *form-
ing a line across the stage.*

The Sergeant returns and calls the roll, bringing
in the names of Corporal Jowler, Mike Donovan,
John Marshall and Willie Marshall. When the
two last are called, soldiers respond, "On guard."
"Local hits" can be made by calling familiar
names, with suggestive responses from the company.

Ord. Attention, Company! Right face! Break
ranks, march.

Exit part of soldiers, leaving JERRY, MIKE, *and
six others on the stage, who seat themselves and sing
camp songs.—The drum beats,* "peas upon the
trencher."

Voice. (*Off,* L.) Fall in for rations.

Mike. D'ye hear that, Corporal Jowler? Why
the divil don't ye lape to yer duty.

Jerry. I wish to thunder, Mike, you wouldn't keep pesterin' me all the time. I shouldn't suppose you thought of anything but eating from morning to night.

Mike. That's because I'm half starved with the mane way ye have of sarving out rations. Faith, I never get more than half what belongs to me.

Jerry. Now that's a gol darned lie. You know that you eat more than any six men in the company.

Mike. Why the divil don't ye go bring thim rations?

Jerry. Who the deuce you talking to? I'd like to know who has command of this squad. (*Exit* L.)

Mike. Stick up for yer rights now, Jerry. Don't let that blasted cook cheat ye because yer only eighth corporal. Faith, its fun jest entirely to see him. "Who commands the squad?" says he. (*Laughs.*) Faith, ye'd think he's a Gigadeer Brindal by the airs he puts on.

Jerry. (*Calling off*, L.) Come along here, some of you fellers, and help lug this stuff up. (*Soldier goes to help.*)

Mike. D'ye hear that now? Some one to help him! I'll bet now I can ate every divil of a bit he's got there.

Re-enter JERRY *and Soldier with rations.*

Jerry. There's yer coffee, help yerselves. (*The men crowd up and fill their cups.*) What in time do ye want to jam up that way for? No need to fill yer cups heaping full, you gol darned hogs. Three hard tack apiece this mornin'. (*Deals them out* MIKE *takes his first, and tries to take a second turn before all are served.*) See here, Mike Donovan, this ain't goin to do no longer. You had your hard-tack once.

Mike. Faith, I thought ye were through with hard-tack, and giving out the salt horse.

Jerry. Ye can all help yerselves to that. But these pertaters I'm going to divide my own self. (*Soldiers sit down. Gives* MIKE *one.*)

Mike. Is this all the prater I'm to have, I dunno?

Jerry That's an all-fired good pertater. (*Gives two to the next, and continues to serve.*)

Mike. See there now, it's two that ye give him.

Jerry. But don't ye see they're a prodigious sight littler than your'n.

Mike. Faith, he has a prater there bigger than mine.

Jerry. Don't ye suppose I know what pertaters be? Ye've got more heft than any man in the mess.

Mike. It's yerself that knows a divilish sight better than that. It's a mane way ye have for getting revenge for that left handed cut I give ye under the right ear. But for all that, ye trate me better than ye do John Marshall.

Jerry. What in thunder have I been doing to John Marshall?

Mike, Faith, now, that's a queer question for the likes of yese to be asking. Isn't it every day that ye kape running to the captain with some blasted lie? And don't I know the reason. Ye'd like to ruin John Marshall because yer love-sick for his wife.

Jerry. Look here, Mike Donovan, ye better be careful how ye talk to me. I guess I know what I'm about. Long as I'm corporal of this company

I calculate to do my duty. Now ye see this is jest the way the matter stands. That feller, Ed Martin, that ye see skulking around the camp here every day, is Mary Marshall's brother, and I suppose the darned critter is my cousin too. Now he's come up here from Virginia, where he owns a nice big place with a lot of niggers, with the excuse that he wants to see his sister, when he hasn't taken notice enough on her for more'n a dozen years to let her know whether he was dead or alive. Now any man that's got half an eye can see what he's here for. He and John Marshall are together purty near all the time, and I've seen some mighty mysterious goings on.

Mike. Ye haven't the least reason in the world to doubt the loyalty of John Marshall. And it's a mane, dirty blackguard ye are for trying to throw suspicion on him.

Jerry. I ain't afeard to tell you nor nobody else just what I think about this ere matter, and I say that John Marshall is a darned rotten-hearted secesh, and you ain't much better.

Mike. (*Springing up.*) Take back thim words now. Take back thim words, I say, or I'll pitch into ye like a thousand a brick.

Jerry. Jerry Jowler ain't in no great habit of swallowing words that he knows are true as gospel.

Mike. (*Taking off his coat*) Will ye be after taking back thim words now?

Jerry. Ye better be plaguey careful what ye do now; it's all-killing dangerous business for a mere private to strike an officer.

Mike. Faith, I'll give ye jist two seconds to take back thim words.

Jerry. Come, dry up, ye gol darned fool, or I'll put ye into the guard house.

Mike. Into the guard house, is it? (*Makes a rush for Jerry, and is held back by the soldiers.*) Jist lave me alone till I get one lick at him, and I'll make him so sick that he'll forget he ever was corporal. Ah! ye maley mouth cur, ye vile scandalizer, if I could only get at ye, it's into mince mate that I'd make ye, mighty quick. (*Struggles, and shouts to be released.*)

(*Enter* CAPT. WINSLOW.)

Capt. Are you at it again, Mike? You'll have to go to the guard house this time.

(*Two soldiers with muskets enter* R. *and take* MIKE *off.* CAPT. WINSLOW *goes with them. The assembly beats, and the stage is cleared of the breakfast dishes.*)

(*Enter Orderly Sergeant,* R.)

Ord. Fall in for company drill.

The men fall in, in one rank across the stage, the line extending off, L. *Four men in citizens' dress enter* R., *with equipments awkwardly put on.*

Ord. (*looking at the recruits.*) Here, Corporal Jowler, you'll have to drill these men.

Jerry. I suppose I can do it. (*Goes up and looks at them with great importance, adjusts their equipments, &c., until the company is marched off.*

Ord. Attention! In two ranks form company. Company right face, quick, march! Right dress! Front! In each rank count twos! Right face! Front! Left face! Front! Order, arms! Shoulder, arms! Support, arms! Shoulder, arms!

3

(*Officers enter* R.) Present, arms! (*Salutes the*
CAPT., *and takes his post.*)

Capt. Shoulder, arms! Without doubling,
right face! Forward march! (*Marches off with
them.*)

Jerry. (*To recruits.*) Come, fall in here, and
I'll see what I can do with ye. Get into a line
here, somehow or other, can't ye? (*Marks with
his foot on the ground.*) There, see if ye can toe
that. Now take the position of a soldier. Spread
out yer toes more. Keep yer heels swag together.
Draw in yer stomachs. Not that way, I mean yer
lower stomach, jest as ye would if ye had the colic.
Hold up yer heads now, no need to look as if ye'd
been stealing sheep. That's a gol darned pretty
way to hold yer guns, ain't it? Don't ye see how
I hold mine? (*Men try to get their guns right.
No. 1 gets his into his left hand, and No. 3 holds
the barrel to the front.*) Hold yer barrels to the
rear. (*Men point their guns behind them.*) Oh!
gol darn it, that ain't what I mean. (*Places guns
in their hands.*) Right, face! (*Nos. 1 and 3 face
left, 2 and 4 right.*) Darnation, that ain't right.
Turn right straight round. (*All. turn directly
about.*) I never did see sich gaumin work in all
my born days. Don't ye know nothin or don't ye?
(*Recruits step around, trying to get the right position.*) There now, see if ye can stand there.
(*Places them front.*) Guess I'll put ye through the
manual of arms. Now I want ye to look right
straight at me, and do jest as I do. (*Hesitates, and
takes off his hat and scratches his head. Recruits
do the same.*) Christopher Chrimus, what ye doin?

(*Throws his hat on the ground. Recruits do the same.*) Jehosephat to Jehosephatation! (*Bringhis gun down. Recruits do the same, striking the butts on their toes. They shout "Oh," kick about, and run off* R.) I'll be darned if I ain't about di.-couraged. Somehow or other I can't seem to get the hang of being corporal. I've just as good a mind to resign as I ever had to eat. Here, Here! where in thunder ye going to? (*Rushes off*, R.)

(*Enter* WILLIE, L. *He takes off his equipments and lays them in the tent.*)

Willie. It isn't much fun to be on guard all night. Let me see, I have only been in camp a little over four weeks, and I already begin to feel like an old soldier. I hope mother will come to-day. Uncle Edward might bring her out as well as not, when he drives from the city. Why, there is Uncle Edward now, I believe. (*Looks* L.) Yes; and there is a lady with him. I believe it is mother. Yes, it is. (*Exit* L.)

Jerry. (*Off* R., *measuring the syllables to correspond with his step.*) Left, left, left—Change yer step. Gol darn it, change yer step. Why don't ye change yer step? Now ye got it—now ye got it. Keep it—keep it. (*Enter with recruits*, R.) Left, left, left. (*Marches off*, L.) Ye darn fool, ye lost it again—lost it again. Halt. (*Drawing out the word with great force.*

Enter MRS. M. *and* WILLIE, L.

Willie. Oh, mother, I am so glad you came. I heard to-day that our regiment was liable to be called any day to march at a few hours' notice, and then I would not have had a chance to see you at

all.   See, here is my tent. (*Looks in.*) I sleep
out in that corner.   Isn't it a nice, cosy little place?
I shan't have no such comfort when I get down
South.

Mrs. M.   Oh! Willie, I don't see how you can
be so gay and light hearted.

Willie.   Ah! mother, I expect to fight the
hardest battle before I go ; and it's only with a
light heart that I can brave the storm.   Come, let
us go out to the parade ground, and see the companies drill. (*Exeunt* R.)

(*Enter* JOHN *and* MARTIN, L.)

Mar.   I think you had better decide, John, to
let Mary go with me.   She will have all the luxuries that my home can afford.

John.   I have no objections, if Mary has not.

Mar.   Well, then that is settled.   I shall probably remain here until your regiment leaves.   Perhaps I may see you down there soon.

John.   It wouldn't be at all strange if you did.

Mar.   Are you really in earnest?   If you are,
I tell you what, you can make a handsome thing
out of this.   We'll lay our plans for it now.   I
will fix it so you can come any time.

John.   It has been my intention to go that way
from the very first.

Mar.   I thought I could not be mistaken.   Give
me your hand.   But it won't do to talk this matter
over here.   We better go where there is no danger
of being overheard.

John.   And when you see me down there, you
will see rows of glittering steel, and bright banners
floating on the air, and on each flag you will see a

star for every State. Edward Martin, if you ever counted upon my disloyalty, you reckoned without your host. But we have been friends, and will not quarrel. As a proof of my friendship I will now give you advice which, if promptly followed, may be the means of saving your life. I do it in strict violation of what I feel to be my duty, but I am willing to take the consequences. You are suspected, sir, of being in league with the Confederate Army, and it is not safe for you to be in this camp another minute.

Mar. I thank you for your timely warning, and will profit by it at once. I should have known that it would not be safe for a Southerner here. I will return at once to the city. I suppose Mary will not wish to go now, and you can provide means for her return.

John. Well then, good-bye, and remember that we bear each other no malice.

Mar. Of course not. Give my love to Mary and Willie. Good-bye. (*Exit* L.)

(*Enter* KATE DONOVAN, L.)

Kate. Oh, Mr. Marshall, is it you? They tell me that Mike is in the guard house, and I believe me heart will break entirely. Oh, what terrible thing has Mike been doing. I walked every step of the way from the city, me heart all the while beating with pride, thinking how noble Mike would look as a soldier, and now I find him confined like a culprit. It must be that he has taken to drink again. It's too bad, it's too bad, after all the strong hopes I had that he was going to mend.

3*

John. This is all news to me, Mrs. Donovan. I was absent from the company this morning. I don't think it can be anything very serious. It is not so terrible as you seem to imagine, to be put in the guard house.

Kate. I don't care so much if he hasn't taken to drink again, for that was all that prevented Mike from being a gentleman. It almost broke me heart, you know, to let him enlist, but he had set his mind upon going with you, and I thought he might receive some of the strength that Heaven had given to you. But I suppose I shall see him soon, for they told me they would send him to his quarters, and this I think is the place. Ah! here he comes now.

(*Enter* MIKE, L.)

Kate. Oh, Mike Donovan, is this the way ye keep the promise ye made to me, when I let ye enlist.

Mike. Ah, Katie, it's drinking whisky that ye think I've been doing. But ye don't know how the Union blue on the outside of Mike Donovan keeps all vile stuff from the inside of him. Wait till ye hear me story, Kate, and then ye'll not blame me. (*Crosses to* R. *of* KATE.) If a mean, dirty blackguard was to hape vile slander upon the name of that man, (*Pointing to* JOHN) calling him a rotten hearted secesh, what would ye have me do?

Kate. If ye didn't walk up and give him a sound drubbing, I'd never own ye for a husband any more.

Mike. Faith, it's jist that same thing I'd done if they'd only let me, and it took a whole regiment to hold me.

John. (R.) Is this really so, Mike? Has any one been making such insinuations of me?

Mike. Yes, and here comes the mane scallawag that did it.

John. Jerry Jowler! Is it possible?

(*Enter* JERRY. L.)

Mike. (*To Jerry.*) Here's the man ye've been scandalizing with yer dirty tongue. Now see if ye've got the courage to spake it to his face.

Jerry. (L.) I don't know what that blasted Paddy has been tellin on yer, but I'll tell ye jest exactly how it is. As a friend, John Marshall, I wouldn't in the least ways harm ye, but as corporal of Co. K, I must do my duty.

Mike. Corporal, corporal, corporal. A devilish fine corporal ye are. Lave me go, Kate, till I get at him, and he'll have more stripes on him than would make him six corporals.

Kate. Hold on till he tells his story, and then ye can go for him.

Jerry. The long and short of the matter is just here ; you are suspected of being a wolf in sheep's clothing, or in other words, that you are an out and out secesh enlisted in this regiment for treacherous designs.

John. (*Holding* MIKE *back.*) No, Mike, don't harm him. The poor fellow is deluded, and don't know what he is doing. Jerry Jowler, I understand all this. I know why it is that you desire my ruin. But I will not judge you harshly, for I doubt not that you are sincere in what you claim to be your duty.   Your mind is warped by this foolish infatuation, that might be excusable in a schoolboy, but ill becoming a man of your years. You might not be willing to own it, you might not hardly be conscious of it yourself, but I know that in your secret heart you would rejoice, should I again be plunged back into the degradation from which I have just been raised.   You know, Jerry, how I was lifted up, how like a miracle the deed was wrought, how Heaven itself seemed to make me its special Providence.   You have heard of the scene at the death-bed of little Minnie, and the vows that were taken there.   And, Jerry, if it should be my fate to fall again, you ought to know the heart of Mary Marshall well enough to know that she would scorn the man that claimed to be her friend and did not bring her proof that he had done all in his power to save me.

(*Enter* Mrs. M., L., *back of characters.*)

Jerry.   That's all very fine talk, Mr. Marshall. I don't know but what you're the noblest man on earth—

Mrs. M. (L. *of* JOHN.)   To me, he is, and you, the vilest. (*Throwing pocket-book at his feet.*) There is your money.   I was intending to return it with thanks instead of scorn.

Jerry. (*Picking up the book.*)   I expected this would be spent for liquor before this time. (*Hesitates, then turns to* Mrs. M.)   Mary—after all—all I've thought—on ye—its—too—too—boo-hoo-hoo. (*Exit* L., *crying very loudly.*)

Mike.   It's divilish little that he lacks of being crazy. (*Cheers off,* R.)

Mrs. M.   What is that?

John.   It is probably the men cheering over some news they have just received.   Perhaps the orders have come for our regiment to move.

Mike.   Faith, I'll go and find out.   Does yer want to go and see the regiment, Kate ?   Come on then.   (*Exit* MIKE *and* KATE, R.)

Mrs. M.   Oh, I hope you will not be called away to-day, John.

John.   It does seem hard to leave you now, Mary.   I know that you have fears for my weakness.

Mrs. M.   Oh yes, John, I have.   The temptation will be so great where you are going.   It seems as if you could not have gone to a worse place.

John.   And I know, Mary, that I could not have gone to a better place.   If anything can inspire nobility in the heart of man, it is the spirit of patriotism and liberty.   There was nothing else under Heaven, Mary, that could have wrought this change in me.   I know I am to leave the influence of home, and be exposed to the peculiar temptations of camp and field.   But wasn't it little Minnie, after all, that lifted me up ?   Wasn't it she, standing at the very gates of Heaven and gazing into those celestial realms, that assured me that our cause was there sustained ?   Wasn't it her angelic voice praising my written words, that seemed to give them the sanction of divine approval ?   Yes; little Minnie was God's own messenger that night.   She was the angel that led me back, and I believe that she will still be near me with her holy influence to keep my spirit undefiled. It may be superstition, it may be a delusion, but it has no less beauty or power if to me it be real. In the weary march; in the silent hours of the bivouac; in the midst of death and carnage; I shall feel her holy presence. And if in the direful confusion, I fall, and breathe out my life unnoticed by a comrade, little Minnie will see me, and her gentle spirit will make it calm as Heaven to me, and I shall die in peace—in glory.

Mrs. M. Oh! John, do not, as we are about to separate, allude to things so terrible.

John. Would you not, Mary, rather have me fall fighting for my country, than return to you the wretch I was a month ago?

Mrs. M. I want you to do your duty, but I do not want you to fall, even though you are again degraded. The world may desert you, and look upon you with disgust and loathing, but Mary Marshall never will.

John. I know, Mary, that you have suffered everything for my sake, and would still suffer until your life was worn away. But this is the resolve I have made: it will not be long before I know if I have strength to withstand the old temptation, and if I am forced to yield, I shall watch for a post of danger, and if demands are made for a heroic sac- rifice, I shall be only too glad to face the death storm, so that I can at least be able to do what only the noblest man on earth can do, die for his country. Then not all the odium that clings to my name can rob it of the laurels with which the na- tion enwreathes the names of all its martyrs.

(*Drum beats*, L.) That call is for the guard. It is probably to be taken off and dismissed to the companies to get ready for the march. I will be back soon. (*Exit* L.)

(*Enter* WILLIE, R., *and takes his gun and equipments from his tent.*)

Willie. These I must return. As the colonel's orderly, I shall not need them. (*Takes paper from his pocket.*) The first order I have to deliver, and little time have I to do it in. Ah! there is mother. She is weeping. She must have heard that the regiment is going to leave. I shall not be able to return to camp again, and this is the last chance I shall have to see her. I hate to bid her good-bye. I can't do it. I would like her parting kiss, but I know how it would be, and I am afraid I should not be fit for the duty I have in hand. It may be wrong to steal away from her, but I believe it will spare pain to us both. (*Music.* WILLIE *watches his mother awhile and then exit* L.)

(*Enter* KATE, R., *and approaches* MRS. M. *slowly.*)

Kate. Has Willie gone without saying good-bye to you?

Mrs. M. Willie gone? Why what do you mean?

Kate. I thought he passed without speaking to you. Poor boy! I suppose he hadn't strength for it. Oh. Mrs. Marshall, Willie has been sent to the city as the colonel's orderly. He is not to come back here, and he is already on his way.

Mrs. M. No! no! Willie would not go away without bidding me good-bye.

Kate. Yes, he has. I know how it was. He dreaded the sight of your tears and anguish. (*Looking,* L.) There, he is mounting his horse now to ride away. There he goes. No; he stops and turns about, he is dismounting—he comes this way. He has relented; he could not go away without his mother's farewell blessing. I will leave; I can't stand here to see that parting. (*Exit* R.)

(*Music. Enter* WILLIE, L.)

Willie. Mother! (*He is impulsively folded in her arms, and gives way to his emotion, and with great effort leaves her. Exit* L.)

Mrs. M. I didn't say a word of what I had to tell him. (*Calling.*) Willie, one moment more. (*Exit* L.)

(*The soldiers off* R. *strike up the John Brown song, and the company marches across the stage, singing.*)

Allegorical Tableau—Emancipation.

ACT III.

SCENE.—*Landscape with set rocks, L.. The Battle-field at midnight. The ground strewn with dead and wounded soldiers of the Union army.* MIKE DONOVAN *and* JAMES MCDONALD *near each other,* C. *Music. Allegorical Tableau:* THE SILENT GRAND ROUNDS.

Mike. (*Raising his head.*) Ah, it's a dismal night is this. See the poor fellows. Sure an what is the reason that no one comes from the hospital to care for the wounded? The place cannot be far from here, but divil a bit can I find the way in the dark. It's no use to try to walk farther with that hole plump through me leg. It can't be that the bones are shivered, and so thim blasted doctors will not be after sawing it off entirely. Faith I think this is a Reb. (*Looking at* MCDONALD.) Divil a bit does he stir. I think he must be kilt outright. Hear the poor fellows groaning. It's nothing that I can do for them. Sure it's weak that I am getting meself. They say there are ladies here in the hospitals, like blessed angels among the wounded and dying. When I heard of it I thought of me own darling Kate. It would be just like her to lend her hand to work like this. Well, I'll sleep till morning, then mebby I'll find me way to the hos-

4

pital, and have these poor fellows cared for. (*sleeps.*)

(*Music. Enter* Mrs. M., R. 1 E. *looking at the soldiers.*)

Mrs. M. Oh, my strength is going, I can hold out no longer. (*Sits on the rocks,* L. 1 E.) If I could only find them. He told me that he heard the roll call of Co. K, and that John Marshall and Willie Marshall were missing. Perhaps wounded, perhaps prisoners, perhaps dead! He could not have been mistaken, for he was the surgeon of the regiment, and his brother an officer in John's company. I should not have left the hospital, for I am needed there. Oh, how terribly faint and sick I am growing! (*Reclines on the rocks.*)

McD. (*Moving.*) Water! water!

Mrs. M. Some one calling for drink. Here, I have some water that I took in case some wounded soldier might want it; but in my own misery, I had forgotten it. Let me remember that other sons and husbands than mine are suffering here. I can care for them, and some kind hand may care for mine. (*Music. She attempts to rise, and sinks fainting.*)

McD. (*Raising himself.*) Can't some of you give me a drink of water? (*Looks at Mike.*) It's a cursed Yankee. I'd die before I'd ask him for a drink.

Mike. And faith, I'd die before ye'd get it of me, and I'm a Yankee from the North of Ireland. D'ye mind that now. So stop your whimpering, for I want to slape.

(*Music.* McD. *draws a knife, and with great effort works himself towards* Mike, *and is about to stab him when* MIKE *rises up and wrenches the knife from his hand.*)

Mike. Ah, ye bloody savage! It's well for ye that I'm a civilized creature, or it's mighty quick that ye'd be sent to Davy Jones' locker. Faith I think it wouldn't be murder at all to kill the likes of ye. Kape still now, or I'll be tempted to do it. (*Aside.*) Faith, I tell him so to scare him; but Mike Donovan could never harm a wounded soldier, though he were ten thousand times an enemy. I would have given him water when he asked me for it, but my canteen has been empty since noon. He's still again. He's dying for water, I fear. Sure, I can't see no human suffer that way, without trying to help him. Mebby I can find some. (*Rises.*) If I only had a crutch now, I could walk with the greatest aise. (*Looks at wound.*) It's only a scratch, after all. (*Touches foot to the ground.*) Och, murder! but it hurts any how. Sure here's a crutch for me. (*Takes a gun and uses it to assist him. Music. Exit*, R. U. E.)

(*Enter* MARTIN *and* LIEUT. WHITE, L. U. E.)

Mar. I think it was somewhere here that he fell.

Lieut. W. It's so cursed dark that ye can't tell one from another. They seem to be all Yanks here. Didn't we mow 'em down though?

Mar. Here he is, but I believe he is dead. (*Bending over* McD. MARY *moves and moans.*) What's that?

Lieut. W. It's a woman. (*Goes up to* MARY.) I reckon it's one of them Sisters of Charity that they have in the Yankee army. She's sick, I reckon. Pretty rough business this.

Mrs. M. Oh, sir, I'm terrible sick. Can't you take me back to the hospital?

Lieut. W. I reckon that depends some on which one ye mean.

Mar. Good Heavens! it is Mary!

Mrs. M. Edward! Brother, this is a strange meeting.

Mar. Strange! I should say it was. What in the world are you here for?

Mrs. M. You should know what I am here for. It is for the work to which the Marshall family is consecrated. A field has been opened where women as well as men can show their love for the Union, and give their lives, if need be, in defending the honor of our flag.

Mar. Then you are an army nurse?

Mrs. M. Call it what you like; I minister to the wounded and dying, and receive their blessings. Some entrust me with a message to their homes on earth, while they bear for me a message to my home in Heaven—the message to Minnie that we love our country more and more, and with our lives will defend it.

Mar. This is a strange fanaticism, Mary; nothing less than superstition. But I should think you would use more prudence. Why, your flesh is burning hot; you have a terrible fever.

Mrs. M. I know it. Oh, take me where I can get something to help me, or I shall die. (*Faints.*)

Mar. Poor Mary! She must be taken to our hospital at once, and then I will make arrangements to have her conveyed to my home. (*Music.* MARY *is taken off,* L. *Exeunt.*)

(*Enter* WILLIE, R. 2 E.)

Willie. It is very strange about father. He was with us all through the battle, and did not disappear until the fighting ceased to-night. Oh, I am so tired, marching and fighting all day in the dust and smoke. I should have rested to-night, but I could not sleep without learning something of father. Oh, how terribly thirsty I am! I have heard of women going over the field, giving cooling drink to the wounded soldiers. Oh, what ministering angels they must be! It seems to me that there cannot be a nobler mission on earth. I have often thought that mother would be just the one to give her service to work like this. Oh, to receive a drink from the hand of darling mother! (*Approaches the canteen that* MRS. M. *has dropped, with her glove clinging to the strap.*) Here is a canteen; but of course it is empty. (*Takes it up.*) No, there is water in it. What is this? A glove —so small—it must be a lady's. That glove! Why, no; what a foolish thought! Well, some woman must have had this in her hand, and while I drink I will imagine that mother left it here for her darling Willie. (*Music. He drinks.*) What was that? It sounded like the voice of Minnie, saying, "Mother did leave it there, Willie." I begin to think that what father says of Minnie may be true. It is no harm to think so. Oh, what holy emotions the thought awakens! All fear and anxiety have left me, and for the first time to-night I feel like sleep. (*Lies down.*) Why need I fear for father, while Minnie watches over him. (*Dreamily.*) Then it did come from the

4*

hand of mother, after all. (*Music. He sleeps. Allegorical Tableau*—THE GUARDIAN ANGEL.)

McD. Water! give me some water!

Willie. What was that?

McD. For God's sake, do give me something to drink, or I shall die.

Willie. (*Going to McD.*) Here, sir, here is some. (*Puts canteen to his lips.*) Where are you wounded?

McD. Here, in the breast. It isn't so bad, the wound; but I was sick before the battle. Maybe I shall die. You're a Federal soldier, but I can't feel hard to you, you look so young. Oh, it's a terrible thing for one like me to die, with a heart black with crime! (*Sinks back.*)

(*Music. Enter* KATE, R. 1 E.)

Kate. (*To Willie.*) Have you seen a lady about here, sir? A friend of mine left the hospital, being so anxious for her husband and son that are missing, they say. She got up from a sick bed, and if not found soon, she'll surely perish.

Willie. Can it be that this is Mrs. Donovan?

Kate. Willie Marshall! and safe from the battle!

Willie. Was it mother that you were looking for?

Kate. Yes, Willie; we both arrived on the field to-day, after the battle commenced. Your mother has made herself sick, and now I suppose she is looking for you and your father.

(*Music.* WILLIE *covers his face in deep emotion.*)

Kate. (*Speaking through the music.*) What is it, Willie?

(WILLIE *picks up the canteen and glove, and hands them to* KATE.)

Kate. (*Looking at them.*) Why, this is Mary's glove, and this is the canteen she took from the hospital. I fear something has happened to her.

Willie. You must go back, Mrs. Donovan, and I will search for mother. Let me have the glove. Keep the canteen; there is water in it yet, and you may find some wounded soldier almost dying from thirst. (*Exit* L.)

Kate. I didn't ask him a word about Mike. I didn't dare to, for fear the worst had happened. Well, I must go back. for it's plenty of work there is for me in the hospital.

McD. Give me another drink. What makes me so cursed dry? (*Sinks back.*)

Kate. Here is some water. (*He drinks without noticing her.*)

McD. Yes, it would make you shudder were I to tell you one half my terrible deeds. Yet the crime that the world may regard as the least, is to me the source of bitterest remorse. Through my influence my sister's husband was brought to ruin. And I did it wilfully, knowing full well the misery it would bring to her who had always been so kind to me. I doubt if she ever suspected me; for as the dark days came upon her, she was kinder than ever to me. But it was only torture. I could not endure it, and for years I have not seen or heard from her. But in the midst of these scenes of death I think of her so often. Only a moment ago, just after you gave me the first drink, I thought I heard her voice. But I suppose my mind must have been wandering. Oh, Kate! If I could only see her once more to ask her forgiveness! (*Sinks back.*)

Kate. His sister's name was Kate! Can it be that it is my brother James? I believe to my soul it is. James! James McDonald!

McD. Oh! curse the dreams! I wish they wouldn't seem so real. (*Looks at* KATE.) Good Heavens! I am not awake yet! Oh, madam, you frightened me. Its so strange to see a woman in a place like this. I was dreaming of my sister, and you seemed just like her, when I saw you.

Kate. You were not dreaming, James; for I am indeed your sister.

McD. Oh, Kate, is it possible? I was just talking about you to the young fellow who gave me the water.

Kate. You were talking to me all the time, James.

McD. He must have left after he gave me the first drink, and it was you that gave me the other.

Kate. Yes, James, I gave you drink.

McD. Then you heard my confession.

Kate I knew it all before, James, and could see that you were sorry for what you had done after it was too late to do any good. When you were suffering by repentance, how could I have the heart to add to your misery by reproaches?

McD. I wish I was deserving the love of such a sister. I am growing weak again. Oh, Kate, don't let me die! (*Sinks back.*)

Kate. I will go and see if I can get him taken to the hospital. (*Exit* R.)

(*Music. Enter Rebel Soldiers*, L., *and carry off* McDonald.)

(*Enter* Mike, R.)

Mike. Faith, I got ye some water, but it took me last bit of strength to do it. Sure, he's gone jist entirely. I was a divilish fool for doing this, any way. (*Lies down where* McDonald *had lain.*) It's set the wound in me leg bleeding so that I'm afraid it'll be the death of me. If I could only be taken to the hospital now, the doctors could fix this. It is hard to be left to die, when a little help could save me. (*Sinks fainting.*)

(*Music. Enter* Kate *and soldiers with stretchers*, R. 1 E. Kate *points to the place where* McDonald *was lying, and goes off*, R. *The soldiers follow with Mike.*)

(*Enter* Capt. Winslow, R., *looking at the soldiers.*)

Capt. They are all dead. I wish we could give them better burial. But if we are driven again tomorrow, there are many poor fellows that will fare worse than these.

(*Enter* Jerry, R., *with spade.*)

Jerry. I guess as how we've got the place deep enough, Captain, and the boys are coming now to take 'em up there.

(*Music. Enter soldiers* R., *and carry off the bodies.*)

Jerry. I thought Mike Donovan was here, somewhere. Must be he's crawled off. And there was a Reb here, too, he's gone.

Capt. I wish we could find John Marshall and Willie. Its singular about them.

Jerry. I don't know nothing about Willie, but I know more about John than I wished I did. Now I've been twitted a good deal about trying to injure John Marshall, and I've been trying awful hard lately to convince myself that I was wrong in my suspicions on him. But what a fellow sees with his own eyes he can't help believing. Now I saw John Marshall when he left the company to-night, and something or other put it into my head to watch him, and what does the fellow do but go right straight into them woods where we had such an all-fired tussle with the Rebs, and take the hat and coat of a Rebel officer, and keep right straight on to the enemy's line.

Capt. Do you expect me to believe this?

Jerry. I'll be darned if it ain't always jest so. Ye won't never believe nothing that I say about him. But I don't care whether ye believe it or not; it's jest as true as thunder. (*Exeunt* R.)

(*Enter* GENERAL COMMANDING, L., *disguised.*

· *Gen.* I've half a mind to go back again. But it's so confounded dark, I suppose it would be impossible for me to find out anything of their position to-night. There is every indication that their troops are being moved to my left, as if to strike me on the flank in the morning. There are some fires now just starting up away off in that direction. That accounts for the rattling I have heard all through the night. It's well for me that I have kept a sharp ear and a watchful eye. Ah, ha! we will just see about this little flanking game. But what if it should only be a feint. What a fool I was for not sending a spy into their lines last night

But then I did not expect this re-enforcement, that now enables me to make a stand. Only for that I should have been miles away before this. (*Looks* L.) Ah, here comes a soldier from the direction of the enemy. It may be an escaped prisoner; if so, I may get some information from him. (*Enter* JOHN.) Hold on a moment, sir. Have you been within the Rebel lines?

John. I don't know as it's any your business if I have.

Gen. Perhaps you are right. But we'll know better about that soon. You don't seem to recognize me.

John. Can this be the General. I beg your pardon, sir.. I should have known you only for your disguise. I will now answer your question civilly. I *have* been inside the Rebel lines, and can give you information that will be of value.

Gen. How happened you to be within their lines? Were you a prisoner?

John. No, General, I entered in disguise.

Gen. For what purpose?

John. To learn all I could to benefit our army. You think it singular that I should undertake such an enterprise upon my own responsibility. I can hardly tell myself why I did. I seemed to be impelled by some secret power.

Gen. (*Incredulously.*) That's rather singular. What do you suppose it was? You don't think it was an angel, do you?

John. (*Seriously.*) Yes, General, I do. But that makes no difference, I want to tell you what I saw there. I suppose, sir, you have noticed signs

of a movement of the enemy to our left. This I
observed as soon as I entered their lines, and
thought I had made a valuable discovery, and
hastened at once to return with the information.
But that was no easy matter, and for hours I beat
about trying to get through. But this was all
Providential, for in my wandering I discovered
that this movement was intended only as a decep-
tion. The noise proceeded from empty army
wagons, and the fires you see off there are burning
houses, kindled purposely to give light. The whole
enemy's force is all massed right down in this
ravine. This feint was of course designed to make
you change your front, when this force, fresh from
a good night's rest, would fall upon your flank, and
annihilate your whole army. I hope you will pardon me for presuming to give advice, but it is
evident that the enemy do not dream of such a
thing as being attacked. But their position is so
clearly defined, that even in the dark you could
march your forces upon them, surprise and rout
the whole army.

Gen. "If this is so, my forces will be moving
down upon them at day-break. What is your
name, sir? (*Takes out book.*)

John. Marshall, John Marshall.

Gen. (*Writing.*) I know a little fellow by the
name of Marshall. He use to be Col. Greene's
orderly.

John. That is my son, sir. He came back into
the company again awhile ago. He prefered to be
with me, and he thought it seemed more soldierly
to carry a gun than to ride about with orders.

Gen. I want to know if you are his father, I got quite interested in him. Now I remember, I have heard the colonel speak of you. There was some interesting circumstance about it. Oh, I know, you were a graduate of Harvard, and started in the profession of Law. I remember now. I am glad I know who you are, for I should hardly want to trust a stranger's story. You might be a spy yourself. No. I can see the resemblance. I shall be very glad to assist you. How would you like a commission? I will find a place for you soon.

John. I thank you very much, General; but I do not desire promotion.

Gen. Don't desire promotion! What is the reason?

John. Its the danger of such a position that makes me shun it.

Gen. Danger! I did not take you to be a man that would think of such a thing, after taking the fearful risk you have to-night.

John. It is not that kind of danger that I fear. There is another enemy than the one our nation is armed against, that I have to fight. One who for centuries has waged continual war upon the whole civilized world, spreading woe and desolation to so many happy homes. You know what I mean, and will understand why I feel safer in the ranks. But believe me, sir, my whole soul is in this work, and if there is any place where I can do more than ordinary service, in an humble way—some dangerous enterprise like the one I have engaged in to-night—I want you to remember me.

Gen. You are a brave man, Mr. Marshall, and

5

for such there is plenty of need. The service you
have rendered to-night is indeed great. Whether
guided by an angel or not, I believe you will be the
means of saving my army from destruction. You
may yet decide to take a commission. When you
do, don't fail to let me know. (*Goes* R., *and meets*
JERRY, *who enters.*)

Jerry. I say, General, if he won't accept that
commission, and ye can't get any other good man
for the place, I shouldn't wonder a darn bit but
what I might be induced to take it myself. I'm a
darn good soldier, especially on drilling recruits.
I had the promise of a commission once; but—
(*Exit* GEN. R.) I say, General, jest hold on a
minute. Perhaps you don't know who I be. That's
jest my luck. Darned if I believe I shall ever get
higher'n a corporal. Hullo, John, is that you?
He didn't offer that commission to *you*, did he?

John. Yes, sir.

Jerry. And you wouldn't take it?

John. No, sir.

Jerry. Ye don't say so. Wall, I swan, if you
an't the darndest queerest critter I ever see. If
he'd offered me a commission, I'd taken it so quick
it would have made his head swim. That's so, by
lightning! But I say, you, there's been kinder
queer goin's on here to-night. Who in thunder do
you think should turn up in the Sanitary corps but
Mary Marshall and Kate Donovan, and both on
'em have been on the battle-field to-night.

John. Mary here to-night! Where is she now?

Jerry. Wall, that's jest what I'm going to tell
ye if ye'll only give me a chance. I've jest been

down to the hospital, and seen Kate, and she told me about it. You see Mary heard that you and Willie were reported in the company as missing. and she got so excited about it, that she started right out to find ye. She was jest about sick abed when she left. When Kate heard on it she was afraid something might happen, so she went right out and tried to find her. She soon come across Willie, who was looking for you, and when he heard about his mother, he put off like mad right away from our lines. I shouldn't wonder a bit but what he run right plump on to the rebels, and got taken.

John.　And how is it about Mary?

Jerry.　Wall, I was going to tell ye about that, if ye'd only give me a chance. You see Ed Martin is here among the Rebs, and came on the field to-night to find one of his comrades that had been wounded. He come across Mary so weak she couldn't walk, and took her into the rebel lines.

John.　How did you learn of this?

Jerry.　Wall, that's what I was going to tell ye, if ye'd only give me a chance. You see Ed had found his comrade, and left him to tend to Mary first, and then sent some men back after him. One of our men fired into 'em when they'se going back, and wounded one. He was left behind and told the story.

(*Enter* WILLIE, L.)

John.　Ah, Willie, you are safe.

Willie.　Have you heard about mother?

John.　Yes; and she is safe, so you must not worry about her any more. It is already growing light, and the day's work will soon begin. The army is to advance and surprise the enemy at an early hour. We must seek our company at once. Before an hour we shall again be engaged in the work of death. We know not which one of us may fall to-day. All may be spared—all may be slain. None but God knows. Willie, have I been faithful thus far to the vow I made?

Willie. Yes, Father, you have.

John. Then if you or Jerry survive me, contrive to let Mary know that I was faithful to the end—that I died like a man. (*Exeunt* R., U. E.)

(*Enter Surgeon and Hospital corps*, R., 1 E.)

Surgeon. This will be a good place. These rocks will shelter us, and we shall be so close upon the lines, that the wounded can soon be brought here. We do not count on any retreat to-day, and it is not likely that we shall be obliged to move. The advance has already commenced on the left. Now follow them up closely, and be ready for work. (*Exit Hospital corps*, L., U. E.)

(*Enter* MIKE DONOVAN, R., 1 E., *with crutch and gun.*)

Surgeon. Hold on here. Where are you going?

Mike. Where am I going? Where the divil should a soldier be after going at this time, but into the fight?

Surgeon. You are in a pretty condition to go into the battle. Look at that leg.

Mike. What the divil is the good of a leg in a fight, but to run with? Faith, its too many nimble legs that ye have in the army already. Haven't I me two hands to handle this with? I'll climb to the top of one of these rocks, and be a sharp-shooter.

Surgeon. You'll go back to the hospital; that's what you'll do.

(*Long roll off* L., *and the firing opens.* MIKE *tries to escape from the Surgeon. A shell bursts on the stage, and the Surgeon runs off,* R. MIKE *mounts the rocks,* L., 1 E., *and fires. The shells continue to burst. The Hospital corps pass* L. *to* R. *with wounded on stretchers. The firing ceases, and* JOHN *is brought in wounded,* L.)

Willie. (*Entering,* L.) Hold, that is father; I want to see him. (*Mike comes up.*)

John. Its nothing dangerous, Willie. Go right back.

Willie. Oh, father, let me go with you.

John. No, Willie; I will be cared for, and you are needed in the battle. Much as I love you, much as I dread to see you go back into that fearful carnage of death, I would have you do your duty like the brave boy that I know you are. So don't let any anxiety for me keep you from your post.

Willie. You are right, father. But if there is anything to make me seem a coward, it is love for you and mother. I will return.

John. Willie, my dear boy, this may be the last time that I shall see you. (*Embraces him.*)

(*A shell bursts on the stage, and all drop.*)

END OF ACT 3.

5*

ACT IV.

SCENE.—*Fallen trees in a forest. Set rock,* R. *Rebel guerrillas discovered seated on the logs, singing.*

(*Enter* EDWARD MARTIN, R.)

Mar. (*To* LIEUT. WHITE, *who rises and salutes.*) Well, what have you had to-day?

Lieut. W. No luck at all, Captain. We have been scouring the country all day, but have discovered nothing. All the Yankee sympathizers seem to have made themselves scarce. They made sorry work of it in trying to arm themselves against the Raven Wings.

Mar. Well, Lieutenant, we have had some excitement since you left this morning. Just before noon a man who lives a few miles north, came riding down at a break neck speed, with the information that a force of Federals had been moving in this direction, and that they were now halted as if for a rest only about ten miles away. Some of the men had commenced scouting about the country, he said; so I sent out Sergt. Jackson with a squad of men, and if he don't nab some of them I shall lose my guess. I suppose you have had a hard march to-day, but if you are not too much

exhausted I would like to have you start at once
for the Federal outposts, and show those Yankee
scoundrels the style of the Raven Wings.

(*The men who have gathered about to listen, cheer
and express their eagerness to go.*)

Mar. Well then, my hearties, away with you;
and let new luster be added to the fame of the
Raven Wings. (*Exit guerrillas with loud cheers,*
L.) They are in their glory now, and woe to the
Federal picket they light upon to-night.

(*Enter* Mrs. M., R.)

Mrs. M. Edward, I have been hunting for you
nearly all the afternoon. I have heard of the
advance of the Union army in this direction, and
it seems like a God-send to me, for I may be able
to reach their lines. It is terrible to live in the
midst of such scenes as daily transpire in this
locality. If I had had the least idea that you
would engage in such work as this, do you think
I would ever have come to live with you here?
But now you must do all you can to get me to the
Union army. If it is moving upon Knoxville we
are right in its line of march, and you will only
have to leave me behind and my object will be
gained.

Mar. Why, Mary, I don't see why you need
complain. You have had all the comforts, and
even luxuries, that my home affords. And though
the Northern army move this way and destroy all
my property here, I shall still have the means to
provide for you. In Richmond, where I intend
you shall go, everything will be as pleasant as you
could wish.

Mrs. M. No, Edward. I do not wish to live any longer in the midst of treason, for it is perfect torture to me to hear and see it, as I am obliged to from day to day. I am made to look with deeper disgust and loathing every hour I remain, upon the work that is going on around me.

Mar. Well, Mary, I will not force you to stay against your will, and if you insist upon it I will aid you all I can. But it is growing dark, now, and you must return to the house; and it will not do for you to venture out so much as you have.

Mrs. M. I know it is imprudent. But I was so anxious to see you in regard to this matter, that I could not wait till your return. I shall depend upon your word and honor now, to help me as I desire. (*Exit*, R.)

Mar. I am sorry for Mary, that's a fact. It was wrong in me to take her here. It causes her a great deal of pain, and her presence unfits me for the duties of my office. Ah! the influence that comes from the heart of a pure minded sister, has no place in the life of one whose heart must be like steel. It is no use to be restrained thus. I have been losing courage ever since Mack has been away, and I am glad that his leave of absence has expired. Ah, there he is now. I knew he would be up to his word. (*Enter* McDONALD, L.) I am glad to see you back, Lieutenant, for we are in great need of you now.

McD. Well, I have had a gay time, Captain, and have come back refreshed and ready for work. What's in the wind now?

Mar. The Yankees are advancing this way,

and are now halted only ten miles above here. Our men are out now, feeling about their lines, and and I expect some of them will soon be returning. I should have gone out myself, only for my sister. It was the worst thing I ever did to get her here. I am not able to be myself while she is around.

McD. Well, I have not had anything to eat since morning.

Mar. You know where to find it. I am going to the house for awhile, and when you get through return here and receive the report of any who may come in. Make them give a full account of what they have done, and if it appears that any one has neglected his duty, you know what to do with him. And there is another thing; some of our men lately have brought in prisoners, not daring to take the responsibility to shoot them down the moment they fell into their hands. The circumstances were somewhat peculiar; but it makes no difference what the circumstances are, if he is a Yankee or a Yankee sympathizer he must have no quarter. And if any one from this army is brought in here alive, I want you to shoot him down the minute you set your eyes upon him, and punish his captors with the utmost severity. Now, remember this.

McD. I will see to it, never fear. (*Exit,* L.)

Mar. I wish I had the nerve and will of that man. It is a great mistake that he is not Captain of the Raven Wings. (*Enter* JOHN MARSHALL, R.) What! John Marshall. How in the name of Heaven came you here?

John. Edward Martin, how in the name of Heaven came you here?

Mar. Why, this is my home; did you not know it?

John. I knew that you lived in Virginia somewhere, but I supposed you would be in the Confederate army.

Mar. Well, so I am.

John. I did not suppose you had any troops in this vicinity except guerrillas.

Mar. Well, perhaps I am what you call a guerrilla. I command an independent organization, called the Raven Wings.

John. What, Edward! Are you the Captain of that inhuman, blood thirsty clan, and is this the neighborhood in which they operate? God help poor Willie, if it is into their hands that he has fallen.

Mar. Good Heavens! what do you mean? Has Willie been captured by my men?

John. He has been taken by some one. We were sent out together this morning for forage, and while we were separated, I heard a shot in the direction of Willie. I started leisurely for the place, thinking as he had doubtless shot something, I would go and see what it was. I searched for him a long time and finding nothing, began to fear that something serious had happened, and pushed on in this direction. I soon found a negro hut, and was told that two rebels just went past with a prisoner who, according to the description I received, must have been Willie. I followed on with all speed, to rescue him if possible. I suppose that in my anxiety and eagerness, I have gone farther than I mistrusted. But it seems to be providential, after

all, for I know that you will see that no harm
comes to him if he is brought to you.

Mar. Did you say they were bringing him
along alive?

John. Of course they would not take him unless
he were alive.

Mar. It will be all right if he's spared until I
see him.

John. If he is spared! What do you mean?
Surely no one would be so inhuman as to murder a
mere child like him in cold blood.

Mar. I hope they will not. No, I feel quite
sure if they started with him alive they will bring
him in safe. But it will not do for you to be seen
here in that dress. You must go to my house at
once, and change it for another. Then if Willie is
brought in here, and it is known that his father
and mother are here, visitors and relatives of mine,
there will be no danger of his being harmed.
There is the house down there at the foot of the
hill. Mary is there now. I would go with you,
but I have business that demands my immediate
attention. (*Exit* John, R.) Now the first thing I
do must be to see McDonald. It will not do to
lose a moment. If such a thing as this should
happen I believe it would kill me. I hope John
will get safely to the house. (*Looks off*, R.) Good
Heavens! there are two of my men out in the
field watching him. They are going to intercept
him. It will be just like them to shoot him.
There is no other way than for me to go with him.
Oh God! it is a terrible strait in which I have
been placed. Willie may be brought in at any

moment, and be shot by my orders. But I will be back directly. (*Exit* R.)

(*Music. Enter* SERGT. JACKSON *and two guerrilas,* L., *leading* WILLIE, *looking very pale and weak. His coat sleeve is stained with blood as if he had received a wound in the arm.*)

Sergt. J. There, my little fellow, we have got to our journey's end for the present. Here is where we always report after our raids.

(WILLIE *lies down. Music—" Who will care for Mother now."*)

(*Enter* McDONALD, L.)

McD. Hullo, what have you here? A little dead Yank? (WILLIE *moves.*) Oh, he's alive, is he? What did you bring him in here that way for? You will have to suffer for this now. The captain has left imperative orders to shoot instantly every prisoner that is brought in alive, and severely punish his captors.

Willie. Oh, sir, do not shoot me. (*Appealing to the* SERGT.) You will not let him, will you? You prevented these men to-day from killing me. Tell him all that I have told you. That I have a mother who thinks so much of me, that she is living in this State. Tell him how much she has suffered ; tell him how little Minnie died, and how father suddenly became changed, and how kind he has been to us all. Oh, sir, you will intercede for me.

McD. Ah, ha! then this is the fellow that is responsible for all this. His case will be attended to directly. (*Aims pistol at* WILLIE.)

Willie. Oh, don't, don't. (*The pistol snaps.*)

McD. Confound the pistol; I never knew it to miss before.

Willie. Oh, spare me now. It was the hand of some good angel that prevented that shot. You surely will not shoot me now.

McD. Perhaps your good angel you speak about will make this pistol miss fire again. Let me try it. (*The pistol snaps again.*) The devil is in it, sure enough. I'll try it once more, and if it don't go, I'll give it up for the present.

Sergt. Oh, Lieutenant, how can you have the heart to do it? I appeal to you in the name of Heaven. Consider his youth, his mother, his father, who is his comrade in arms. If you could hear his story, how his life so long dark has recently been lighted up. How his young heart glows with bright hopes just kindled there. Oh, how can you shoot down in cold blood one so young and fair?

McD. That's a fine speech, and here is the reward. (*Shoots the* SERGT. *dead.*) The good angel didn't stop that, did it, my little covy? Now we'll try it once more on you. (*Fires at* WILLIE, *who receives the shot in his side, groans, and sinks back.*) That don't quite fetch him, I guess. This will settle him. (*Points pistol close to his head.*)

(*Enter* MARTIN, R., *and stops him.*)

Mar. Hold! Great Heavens! do you know what you have been doing? This is Willie Marshall, my sister's only child. Oh, you villain, you have killed him. (*Grasps* MCDONALD *by the throat.*)

6

McD. Hold on, Captain, this is no way to treat a man for strict obedience to orders.

Mar. I know it, I can't tell what I'm about. It's all my fault. Oh God, what will Mary say? He is not dead. What do you stand staring there for, men? Why don't you run and get him something to drink, and dressing for his wound? (*Exit men, l..*) Willie, Willie Marshall.

Willie. (*Opening his eyes.*) Uncle Edward, is it you? Is mother with you?

Mar. No; but I expect she will be here soon.

Willie. She will dress my wound when she comes, and if they will let her take care of me, perhaps I will get well. No one could ever tend me like mother. Oh, how weak and faint I am.

(*Soldiers return with a dish of water, a flask of brandy, bandages, &c.*)

Mar. (*To one of the men.*) You go to the house, and have my sister come here immediately. Now run for your life. (*Exit Soldier, r.*) Now, Willie, take a drop of this, it will give you strength. (WILLIE *drinks from the flask.*) Where is your wound?

Willie. Here, in the side. I was wounded in my arm, too, before I was taken, but that is not so bad as this.

Mar. (*Examining the wound in his side.*) Oh, see the blood! Hand me some of that cloth. (*Fixes the wound.*) There, that will stop the bleeding some. Have some more drink. Here is some water.

Willie. Do you belong with these men, uncle Edward?

Mar. Yes, Willie, I am their captain.

Willie. Their captain! Was it then by your orders that I was shot?

Mar. Yes, Willie, I did leave orders to have all shot that were brought in alive. It is the common practice of all bands like ours. We do it that we may be able to wield greater power in repelling invasion. But I did not once dream that you would be taken. Oh, I feel as if I were your murderer, and you must regard me as such.

Willie. Oh no, uncle, I do not indulge in any thoughts of the kind whatever. It was only a mistake, and I am sure you have been very kind to me, and are doing all you can for me now. Oh, if you had only been here when I first came, you could have saved me, couldn't you?

Mar. I hope I did come soon enough to save your life. Your mother will soon be here, and she will dress your wound, and we will arrange something and take you to the house. I don't believe your wound is very dangerous.

Willie. It's no use to hope. I am growing weak fast, and cannot hold out much longer. But I want to see mother before I die. Why don't she come?

(*Sinks back. Music—" Who will care for mother now."*)

(*Enter* Mrs. M., R.)

Mrs. M. Oh, Willie, my darling boy, they have murdered him. Poor innocent child, it seems but yesterday that I held him to my breast and listened to his childish prattle. So young and childish, how could they shoot him so? Oh, Willie, tell me who has been so cruel to you. Look up to me, darling, it is I, your mother.

Willie. Oh, mother, they would shoot me, although I begged so hard for them to spare me. I told them all about you, all about father and Minnie. I told how much you loved me, for I thought that perhaps they might know something of a mother's love, and that I might gain their sympathy. One of them did intercede for me, and he was shot down for it. Oh, mother, I don't believe you can do anything for me. It's a terrible wound.

Mrs. M. Who was it that shot you after you were brought here?

Willie. That is the one. (*Pointing to* McD.)

McD. I did it by your brother's orders, Mrs. Marshall.

Mrs. M. Edward Martin, is this so?

Mar. No, Mary, not as you understand from him. Oh God, don't make it any worse than it is. Oh, Mary, I believe it will kill me. (*To* McD.) Why don't you tell her just how it is, don't you see that I can't do it myself? ·

McD. Well, all there is about it is that Captain Martin gave me strict orders to shoot instantly every Yankee that was brought in here alive. He said it didn't make any difference what the circumstances were, to spare the victim on no condition whatever. If his orders had not been so imperative, I think I should have spared the boy after his earnest appeal to me. But I always make it a point to obey orders. Have I told it about straight, Captain?

Mar. Yes, it is all true. I am responsible for the whole. Oh, that the lightning from Heaven would strike me dead.

(*Enter* Lieut. White *and guerrillas.*)

Lieut. W. We are closely pursued by some Yankee troops. They are almost upon us.

McD. How large is the force?

Lieut. W. There cannot be a great many of them. I think it would be well to make a stand here.

Mar. Lieut. McDonald, you take command. I am fit for nothing now.

McD. All right. Now, men, get shelter behind these logs and stumps, and fight like tigers.

(*The men take positions for defense, passing over the form of* Willie, *and crowding* Mrs. M. *to the* R. Martin *stands in a sort of stupor in front*, L. C. *Union soldiers fire off* L., *and* Martin *falls.* Mrs. M. *goes off*, R. *The fire is returned by the Rebels, and kept up for awhile on both sides. The Rebels fall back to the* R. Willie *and one of the wounded rebels are carried off*, R. *The dead are left where they fall. The Union troops,* "Co. K," *appear* L., *firing. The Rebels return the fire off* R., *and some of the Federals fall. The rest shout and charge across the stage.*)

Mar. (*Raising his head.*) Our men are routed sure enough. I wonder how Willie is. I mus' try and get to him. I may yet be instrumental in saving his life. Oh, God! how I bleed.

(*Music. He crawls towards the place where* Willie *lay, and where a Union soldier now lies on his face. He turns him over.*)

Mar. No, it is not Willie; but he looks as

6*

young and as fair. His lips move, he whispers, "Mother." It is somebody's darling. (*Music.— "Somebody's Darling.*") Hear him breathe the names of dear ones at home. Ah, my poor boy, no mother or sister can hear you. They are hundreds of miles away. God help them when they hear of this. Oh, I am growing weak! Where is Willie? I must find him while I yet have strength. (*Music. Attempts to move, but sinks exhausted.*)

(*Enter* Mrs. M. *and* John, R. *The latter as a guerrilla.*)

Mrs. M. This is the place. Here is Edward.

Mar. Mary, is it you? I have been trying to find Willie, but my strength has failed me.

John. (*Approaching.*) Edward Martin!

Mar. Oh, John, don't curse me. I have been very cruel; I have brought you this terrible affliction; but it was not intentional. I tried my best after you came to prevent it. I could have done it had I not been obliged to go with you. No, John, I have never wilfully wronged you in thought or deed; for I always loved you like an own brother.

John. Don't talk that way, Edward, I bear you no malice. I do not entertain one hard thought towards you. I understand it all. Where is Willie?

Mar. I don't know. He was lying here. I thought that wounded soldier there was he; but it is not. (*Search is made for* Willie.) Can't you find him? Then some of my men must have carried him off.

John. Where do you think they would take him?

Mar. To Richmond. We intended to fall back there when your army advanced.

John. Then I will follow in that direction. I can pass to-night as one of your men. God may help me to find Willie, and save him yet.

Mar. You are not going, Mary. You will not leave me here to die all alone. I know I am not worthy a sister's care, but I am in such misery.

John. No, Mary, it will be impossible for you to go with me, and you are needed here. I must be off at once. There is danger before, and this may be our last parting. Good-bye, Edward; remember that I hold nothing against you. May God restore you to health. Good-bye, Mary; I shall not go alone. The same bright angel that I so often have seen in the lone silent hours of the bivouac, will be with me still. Good-bye. (*Exit* R.)

Mar. See if you cannot do something for this poor fellow, he is moaning so piteously, and calling for his mother.

Mrs. M. Oh, how he looks at me with his glazing eye! See him grasp my hand. He thinks I am his mother. What a heavenly light beams in his face. He is dead. Poor boy, did you die thinking that your own darling mother was bending over you? Then this shall be her farewell kiss. (*Music—" Let me kiss him for his mother."*) If Willie dies like this, who will give him the farewell kiss of mother? (*Two shots off*, R.) What can be the matter now?

Mar. Perhaps John has been mistaken for an enemy by his own men, and fired at.

Mrs. M. Oh, then they have killed him! God help me, if they have!

(*Enter* John *hastily, as if pursued.*)

Mrs. M. Oh John, you are safe. Were you fired at?

John. Yes, but I was not hit.

Mike. (*Off* R.) Be aisy now, I have a bead drawn on him.

Jerry. (*Off* R.) Gol darn it, hold on. Don't ye know nothing or don't ye? You allfired gauming Irishman, that's a female woman.

Mike. Away wid yer blarney. Its not her at all at all that I'm aiming at.

Jerry. Wall, they're so slapping close together, ye can't tell which ye may hit. We can take him now without shooting him.

(*Enter* Jerry *and* Mike, R.)

Jerry. John Marshall! and Mary too! Was it you, John, that we fired at just now? Where were you going?

John. I was going in search of Willie.

Jerry. Now, John Marshall, what ye have been telling me may be true as gospel. But I must say that it does have kinder of a scaly look to me. Now, Mike Donovan, what did I tell ye? When the Marshalls came up missing this morning I knew there was something in the wind; cos I knew that Ed Martin lived somewheres here abouts. You understand now how the guerrillas got scent of us, and if it hadn't been for me mistrusting what's up, we'd have been caught napping, jest as true as the world. Now, Mike, ye know how ye'd never believe what I said about this thing ; but now its all before your eyes as plain as broad daylight. There lies Edward Martin, captain of the guerrillas, and there stands John Marshall, and ye see how he is dressed, and you know where he was trying to go jes now, when we fired at him. As a friend, John Marshall, I wouldn't in the least ways harm ye ; but as corporal of Co. K., I must do my duty. You stand guard here, Mike, while I go for the captain and he shall see the thing jest as it is.

Mike. Jerry Jowler, ye haven't half heard his story ; and if what ye suspect be true, why can't we let him off. If its to the captain ye are going with that message, ye'll have to walk over the dead body of Mike Donovan. (*Raises his gun.*)

John. I will tell you just how it is. Willie was captured this morning by guerrillas, and I followed in pursuit, till I reached this place, and found Edward Martin. He took me to his house, and promised that he would prevent harm falling to Willie. He told me to change my clothes, so that I would not be in danger from his men. Willie was brought to this place, and shot by one of the guerrilla officers, as he had been previously ordered by the captain in case any one should be brought in alive. Our company then advanced, and Willie was taken by the guerrillas in their retreat. I came here from the house after the fight, and finding that Willie had been carried away, I resolved to follow him and do all I could to save him. I had just started when I encountered you.

Mar. (*Who has been listening.*) Jerry Jowler, you will not doubt the word of a dying man.

Then hear me swear before God, that all he said
of what transpired between him and me is true as
Heaven. I have sounded the heart of John Marshall; I have tried to tempt, tried to bribe him,
and I believe no power on earth can make him
violate in deed, in word, in thought, or in spirit,
the promise he made to his dying Minnie.

Jerry. Wall, Edward, some how or other I can't
help believing you. I am brought to my senses at
last. What a gol darned fool I have been. Now,
Mike Donovan, I am jest the chap that'll go snucks
with ye, on anything ye'll undertake to save little
Willie.

Mike. Then, with God's leave, we will all
three start this blessed minute on the road to Richmond.

John. Yes; four of us. I never forget the
bright angel that God sends to guide my steps, and
keep my spirit undefiled.

Mar. There; she is waiting for you now. You
do not see her there? Oh, how beautiful!

*(Allegorical Tableau shown behind the scene as
the curtain falls.)*

ACT V.

SCENE.—*Same as Act 4.*

(*Enter* MRS. MARSHALL *and* KATE, R.)

Mrs. M. This is the place where Willie was shot. That was nearly a year ago.

Kate. Then it was here that you saw the last of Mike. It is strange that nothing can be heard from them.

Mrs. M. Not so very strange, for it was a dangerous mission they started upon. Poor Willie, he could not have lived long after he left here, for he had a terrible wound in the breast. It is torture to think that he must have died all alone, to be buried in some desolate spot. Even the solace of visiting his last resting place, and strewing his grave with flowers, is denied me. The rest may have been taken prisoners. That is all the hope I have left. But the chances of surviving the tortures of those Southern prison pens are indeed small.

Kate. Then you have been here ever since that night.

Mrs. M. Yes; I told John that I would wait until he returned. And I can't bear the thought of leaving until I hear something from them. This place has been in communication with the North ever since that night. I have heard from the regiment several times, and nothing is known of them there.

(*Enter* JAMES MCDONALD, L. *The ladies start with fear.*)

McD. Don't be frightened, ladies. I'm not a bear, that I'll eat ye up. What! By my soul, if there isn't Kate again.

Kate. Brother James! Oh, I am so glad to see you. I did not know but you died that night after I left you. I went to the hospital after some men to bring you in. I pointed out the place where I supposed you laid; but when the men came into the hospital, it was my own husband, Mike, that they had in place of you. And, James, he told me how it happened. He said he had been lying beside you, and I suppose you must have got wild like, for he said you attempted to kill him because he couldn't give you water. Then after that he took pity on you, and though he was wounded so that he could hardly walk, he started to try and find you something to drink. It was while he was gone that I saw you. Then after I left you he returned, weak from the loss of blood, and found you gone. He sank fainting in the very place where you had lain, and was taken in your stead. And the young fellow who gave you the drink before I did, was Willie Marshall.

McD. (*Drawing* KATE, L.) Ask that woman to leave, I don't want her here. I've got something to say to you. (KATE *goes to* MARY.) It is Mrs. Marshall, the mother of the boy I killed. (*Exit* MRS. M, R. KATE *returns.*) Wasn't that Mrs. Marshall?

Kate. Yes.

McD. Do you know about her boy being shot here ?

Kate. Yes ; she told me all about it.

McD. I was the man, Kate, that murdered him.

Kate. What ! James McDonald, kill that noble young boy, after he begged you over and over again to spare him. Oh, James, I knew you were bad and wicked, but I didn't think you were cruel enough for that.

McD. I am cruel enough for anything, Kate. But I believe this thing will be the death of me yet. It gives me the horrors half the time. Do you know, Kate, that I believe that murdered boy haunts me.

Kate. Oh, James, don't talk so ; it makes me shudder.

McD. Its the truth, and I am made a coward by it. The men all know it, too.

Kate. Its only your imagination, James.

McD. No, no, it isn't so. I wish to God it was. Let me tell you one thing that happened. When I was acting as scout, I had in my room one night important dispatches locked in a valise. Some time in the middle of the night I awoke. The room was light, and I saw some one at the table, and he seemed to be copying from the dispatches. His features were turned towards me, and I recognized Willie Marshall. I covered my face in horror, and lay trembling all the rest of the night. In the morning I found the dispatches safe where I had left them, and I thought it must have

7

been some horrid nightmare or something of the kind. But I afterwards learned that a literal copy of those dispatches had been carried to the enemy. Other similar cases have occurred. He has also been seen by my men. Oh, it is terrible! (*Shudders.*) This is the first time I have been here since he was killed. And the 'sight of his mother—Oh, Kate! I wish I had died that night you saw me on the battle-field.

Kate. Oh, don't talk so; think of something else. How does it happen that you are here?

McD. I came here in search of a spy. He is an old man, or some one disguised as an old man. He has carried important information from our army to the Yankees several times. We have been completely deceived by him, but at last he was detected, and a large reward is offered for his capture. I have got on his track, and I think he has come this way. I was going to Martin's house. My men were ordered there by different routes, so I had better be there myself to prevent their committing any depredations. (*Exeunt* R. *Music. Enter* JOHN, JERRY *and* MIKE, L, *pale and emaciated.*)

John. (*Sinking upon the ground.*) It's no use, I can't go any farther. My strength is all gone.

Mike. Faith, I don't much wonder. Its not a very good chance that it was to raise muscle down there in Libby. But ye were sick with fever when ye left. Sure its a wonder that ye ever walked a mile. Divil a bit have we had to ate since we started. I don't see what has put the strength into ye.

John. It was the yearning for the sight of the loved ones at home. But I have given up now, I have given up. Go along without me. Let me die here.

Jerry. John Marshall, we ain't going to do nothing of the kind whatsumever. Ever since that night I was brought to my senses, hain't I stuck to ye like a brother?

John. Yes, Jerry, you have. I know that only for your rash attempt to rescue me, you would never have suffered in that loathsome prison.

Jerry. And if you imagine that I'm going to desart ye now, you are teetotally and everlastingly mistaken. I believe if we hadn't kept in the woods and fields all the way, and gone to some of the houses and got something to eat, it would have been a darned sight better for us.

Mike. If we'd done that we'd got gobbled up long ago. Its a divilish sharp eye that they're kaping on these fellows escaping from prison.

Jerry. Somehow or other this place looks kinder natral. Darned if I don't believe this is the very spot where we had that fight with the guerrillas. I say, didn't Ed Martin have a house near by here?

John. Yes.

Mike. And it wouldn't be strange at all if Mary was there this blessed minute.

John. It isn't likely that she would stay there so long.

Mike. Don't ye be too sure of that now. Didn't she say she'd wait until we came back?

Jerry. Look here, John, it isn't but a little ways down to the house. Can't ye muster up strength enough to go? I don't suppose I can help ye a darn bit, for its all I can do to crawl now. I guess its about the same with you, ain't it, Mike?

Mike. Faith, yer right. It never agreed with me to go without ateing. Me appetite was always a dale of trouble to me. Do you remember, Jerry, the fuss I made over that prater? Faith, wouldn't I like to see that prater now?

Jerry. We didn't know what hard times was then, did we, Mike? I say, John, I've got a little brandy here in a bottle. If ye'll take some of this, it may give ye strength to get down to the house.

John. No, no, take it away. Haven't I pledged myself never to touch it?

Jerry. But this 'ere is different. I wouldn't offer it to you under no circumstances, John, if I didn't think yer life depended on it.

John. I prefer death to the violation of that vow registered in Heaven. Why don't you go on? Its no use trying to save me.

Mike. Wasn't it both of us that said we wouldn't leave ye as long as ye lived. Faith, it's meself that took the same vow ye did, and God knows that thus far I've kept it. But if I was in your place, I should think it me duty to take anything that would put strength into me.

John. Jerry, Mike, are you determined to stay with me, and thus throw away your lives?

Jerry. John Marshall, you talk about vows, and their being registered in Heaven. Now haven't we all sworn to stand by each other until we were safe beneath the Old Flag?

John. Let me take the bottle. Do you think this would give me strength?

Jerry. There ain't much doubt about that. That stuff will revive a man wonderfully, when he's weak like you.

John. Would to God, it would do nothing more. Well, for your sake, I will drink it. (*Raises the bottle.*) No, no, I can't. I seem to see the imploring face of that dying girl, pleading with tearful eyes for me not to touch it. No, Minnie, darling, I won't do it. No, I won't.

Mike. (*Looking* L.) Ah, d'ye mind that, Jerry?

Jerry. It's rebs, just as sure as I'm alive.

Mike. And they're coming this way.

Jerry. No, they're cutting across towards the house. But they'll come plaguey snug to us, and if we don't lay pretty darned low they'll see us, and then we're gone suckers. There, they've got by.

Mike. They're after us, sure. We must be after hiding somewhere. Come, John, take a drink of the brandy.

John. Won't you go without me?

Jerry. I kinder kalculate we won't.

.(*Music.* JOHN *raises the bottle slowly to his lips and is about to drink, when* MARY *enters,* R., *and dashes it away.—Picture.*

Jerry. Ain't any of ye ever going to speak. Don't be frightened, Mary; he hasn't touched a drop on it. Ye see, he was going to drink it to give him strength. He wouldn't do it no how to save himself. But ye see, Mike and I were bound not to go along without him, and he was doing it jest to save us.

Mike. Faith, and I think it was a divilish mane thing in us, anyway, for allowing him to do it.

Mrs. M. How does it happen that you are here in this terrible condition?

John. We are refugees from Libby prison in

Richmond. We escaped nearly a week ago. The night we left here in search of Willie, we were taken prisoners, and have been confined ever since.

Mrs. M. Have you ever heard anything about Willie?

John. Not a thing. Have you ever heard from the regiment?

Mrs. M. Yes; nothing is known of him there.

John. Then he must be dead. Poor Willie! I had hoped that he might have survived.

Mike. Mrs. Marshall, is it anything that ye've heard of Kate?

Mrs. M. Yes, Mike; she is here now stopping with me. She is down there in the house with her brother, James.

Mike. Faith, that puts more strength into me than a whole barrel of brandy, or whiskey aither. I'll go right down there this blessed minute.

Jerry. See if ye can't find something to eat down there.

Mike. Divil a bit will I forget that.

Mrs M. Yes, have Kate bring some up as soon as possible.

John. Mary, the vow has not yet been broken. For four years I have fought the enemy that would ruin our country, and struggled with the demon that would destroy the peace of our home. For four years the bright angel has watched over me, for four years I have been a man.

(*Shots off* R.)

Mike. (*Off* R.) Faith, ye dropped two on 'em, but the rest are after you. (*Enters.*) Come right this way now, and I'll hide ye and put them off the track. (*Enter* WILLIE, *disguised as an old man, and* MIKE *throws a blanket over him, next to the rock,* R. 1 E.) It's a Union man that he is, hunted down by the Rebs. Here they come after him now.

(*Enter* JAMES McD., R.)

McD. Mike Donovan, is that you?

Mike. Jim McDonald, for the sake of Kate I'll take yer hand.

McD. I am in pursuit of an old man, that we suspect is a spy. Have any of you seen him?

Mike. Yes, I seen him. There he goes now, running like the divil. Ye better hurry up, or ye'll lose him.

(*Enter Guerrillas,* R. -1 E.)

McD. Here, men, fall in right here, in one rank. Are all your guns loaded? (*Men respond. He goes down the line, and whispers to each man.* KATE *enters,* R.) Ready, aim! (*The men aim at the blanket.*) Now, sir, my fine fellow, we've got you. Six loaded muskets are aimed at you; and, unless you rise and surrender, we shall fire. You have shot two of our men already, and it will not do for you to tempt us further. Come, sir, rise and show yourself.

(*Music.* WILLIE *throws off the blanket, and appears without the disguise.* McDONALD *and his men stand appalled.*)

Mrs. M. Willie Marshall!

Willie. Here I am, all safe and well. Father, what is the matter with you?

John. Nothing, Willie, only worn out with fatigue and hunger.

McD.   Alive!   Willie Marshall, do you remember me?

Willie.   Yes, sir, you were the man that shot me that night.

McD.   I will not ask you to forgive me.   But if God will spare my life, I will show you and your parents that I am penitent.   Mike and Kate, I have wronged you both, but I know that you will help me to become an honest man.   The first thing I do towards reformation will be to denounce the Southern Confederacy.   Then, with my company, I will see that you and your friends are safe beneath the Old Flag.

(*Enter* LIEUT. WHITE, L.)

Lieut. White.   Captain McDonald, you are ordered to report immediately to Gen. Mosby. Lee has surrendered the Army of Northern Virginia, and Mosby's men are to give their parole with the rest.

John.   Lee surrendered!   Then the war is virtually ended.   Ah! this gives me strength.

McD.   Do you hear that, boys?   The Southern Confederacy has gone up.   Now every one of you, three cheers for the Union.   (*The cheers are given.*)

John.   Thank God, the carnage of blood is ended, and Peace will soon spread her bright wings over a land free from the curse of Slavery.

Mrs. M.   And happiness will dwell once more in a home free from the blight of intemperance.

(*Exeunt* R.   *Allegorical Tableau.*)

www.ingramcontent.com/pod-product-compliance
Lightning Source LLC
Chambersburg PA
CBHW030001030726
47499CB00008B/2850